A story for
you. Rick McNan

The Last unicorn on the prairies

written by Rick McNair

illustrated by chris Mcvarish-younger

GREAT PLAINS
PUBLICATIONS

Great Plains Publications
420 – 70 Arthur Street
Winnipeg, MB R3B 1G7
www.greatplains.mb.ca

Great Plains Publications gratefully acknowledges the financial support provided
for its publishing program by the Government of Canada through the Book
Publishing Industry Development Program (BPIDP); the Canada Council for
the Arts; the Manitoba Department of Culture, Heritage and Tourism; and the
Manitoba Arts Council.

Design & Typography by Gallant Design Ltd.
Printed in Canada by Friesens

CANADIAN CATALOGUING IN PUBLICATION DATA

Main entry under title:

McNair, Rick
The last unicorn on the prairies

ISBN 1-894283-36-8

Unicorns – Juvenile fiction.   I. Title
PS8575.N33L37 2002   jC813'.54 C2002-910620-6
PZ8.2.M36La 2002

I is me, but sometimes you,
   I will tell you a story that pretends to be true.

Once beside a time that was dark just before it was light,
Red Rooster got ready to announce the sun.
He checked to see if he was looking
good and headed for the top rail of
the fence to sing up the sun.

Red Rooster took a big
rooster breath and let
his cry fly:

Moooooo

Silence.

"Who said Moo?" asked the farmer with a wrinkle on his face and he looked right at Red Rooster. "It should be Brown Cow that said moo but it's you who said moo, Red Rooster, it's you!"

But that is the last part of the story and we haven't even done the first part.

Clyde the Horse told me this story.

I asked Clyde how a rooster could moo and he said he would tell me this tale.

"Are you going to sell me your tail?" I asked.

"Tell, not sell and tale, not tail," said Clyde.

I new, I mean, I knew the difference between tell and sell but not tale and tail. So Clyde sang:

> The tail I wear is good to swat flies,
> The tale I tell has a big surprise.

So let me tell you the tale that Clyde told me. Clyde should know since he was there AND I should know since he told me AND you will know since I am telling you AND you can tell it to somebody new.

Clyde said Red Rooster went Mooo! It was right after chasing the Last Unicorn on the Prairies. So let's go back in the story to just before that Unicorn.

All the animals at the McNair farm heard two important things. One was that the farmer was running out of money and he might have to sell the farm. The animals did not want that because they might lose their jobs.

The second and most surprising thing was that there were fresh unicorn tracks in the pasture, right where the cattle were having a grass salad.

For the few of you that don't know what a unicorn looks like, listen to this handy unicorn watcher's song:

A Unicorn looks like a little grey horse,
With a waving tail like a lion of course!
But what's most important for you to know?
One diamond hard horn on her head does grow,
One single sharp horn with a bright coloured glow!

Now all the animals knew that if you catch a unicorn you would find gold or get a wish. Or something that is really good.

Clyde wasn't sure this was true. He just wanted to see a unicorn. He was sure he was some kind of relative of the unicorn. Maybe a second cousin twice removed.

They called a meeting. Red Rooster was in the chair. After a lot of scratching and barnyard noise, someone from the back of the meeting yelled out…

"Let's find the unicorn and get a treasure of gold!"

So five animals volunteered to hunt for the unicorn.

Red Rooster er er err err eerrrrrrrrred!

Black Cat meowed loud. Lee.

Spotted Dog barked bow wow,

And moo moo said Brown Cow.

Clyde the Horse went too, just to meet his distant relative.

The band of five went to where the tracks of Unicorn began. Right there in the middle of the pasture.

How did the tracks start right in the middle of a field? Clyde didn't tell me and I haven't figured it out yet.

The five waved goodbye and started their journey to find Unicorn and a golden treasure. Look, and you will see…

A journey that they all knew would be full of…
ADVENTURE! DANGER! COURAGE! MYSTERY!
And they hoped, TREASURE!

Everyone but Clyde wanted to be boss so they all talked at once.

They sounded like a TV that couldn't stop changing channels.

With all that noise, everything and anything that heard them ran away. Even some that could not run tried to escape that babble. There was no way the farmyard five could sneak up on anything. Especially a unicorn.

"Quiet!" said Clyde.

Nobody could hear with all that yelling.

"QUIET!" said Clyde. "We made so much noise we even scared away the clouds. If we don't get quiet quickly we will never find Unicorn."

When they heard this the rooster, the cow, the dog and the cat said:

Er er er er er er!

Mooo!

Bow Wow!

Meow!

And all the birds and frogs and rabbits, flew, hopped, and ran away. Even some prairie flowers tried to leaf, I mean leave.

So "BE QUIET" said Clyde.

And they were.

"What can we, meow, do?" asked Black Cat.

"If we want to sneak up on Unicorn we will all have to be quiet," hoarsed Clyde.

"SO?" said all.

"So, we have to be very, very, quiet," whispered Clyde.

"HOW?" said all.

"We just take all our voices out and put them in a voice box," smiled Clyde.

The only place this could happen is in our story. Lucky for us that is where it happened.

So the farmyard five, carrying the voice box, mimed their way across the prairies. No talking out loud, they could only make signs, signals, and funny faces instead of words.

They followed the hoof prints of Unicorn up and over, under, around between backwards and through the prairies.

And

And

And

And

And

And

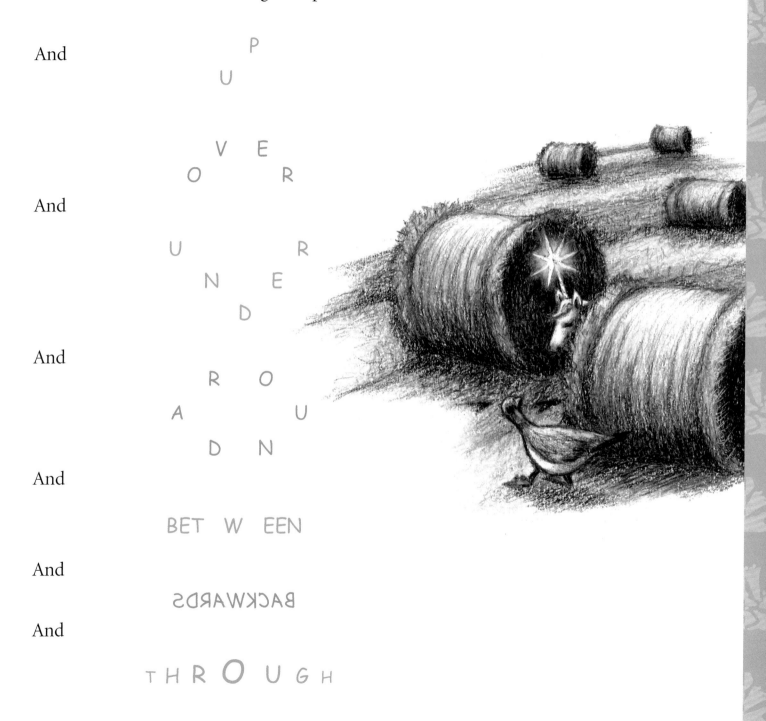

P
U

O V E R

U R
N E
D

R O
A U
D N

BET W EEN

BACKWARDS

THR O U G H

On and on they went, following the hoof prints of Unicorn.

They went up the hill of prairie flowers.

They went over the bridge that crossed the creek.

They went under the one big tree
at the edge of the road.

They went between the blue flax and the yellow canola.

They went backwards in the field of wheat.

They went through the field of tall sunflowers.

Up and over, under, around, between, backwards and through!

If you want to get there, that is what you do.

Up and over, under, around, between, backwards and through!

If you will follow me, then I will follow you… too.

They had gone for three days and three nights and I don't know how many ups and overs, unders, arounds, betweens, backwards and throughs. But I know they did at least as many as there are robins in the spring and geese in the fall.

They were getting very close to the end of the trail. The five could tell this by the signs. The hoof prints were getting fresher and heading into that small wood on top of Duck Mountain.

So they had to get their final plan ready.

They mimed this way and they mimed that way and finally they figured out what you would have told them if you were there.

They figured out that they would get all around Duck Mountain Woods and, on silent signal, mime their way into the woods and go straight on till they got to the middle of the woods where Unicorn would be.

"Remind me what a unicorn looks like," signed Brown Cow.

Rooster gave a mime signal and all together like a silent band,
they mimed this very song to the cow:

> *A Unicorn looks like a little grey horse,*
> *With a waving tail like a lion of course!*
> *But what's most important for you to know?*
> *One diamond hard horn on her head does grow.*
> *One single sharp horn with a bright coloured glow!*

bright glow

sharp horn

little grey horse

tail like a lion

So on the signal they all mimed into the woods, where the unicorn hoof prints lead.

With no sound and hardly a sight they wiggled and waggled and wormed and womped toward the centre of the woods.

With a step and a hop and a jump and a hide they got closer.

And closer.

      And closer.

          And closer.

And really, really close…

To the middle of the woods.

And they looked and they saw…

NO UNICORN!

BUT!! THEY SAW…

A little grey horse,
With a wavy tail like a lion of course.

And one big black top hat right in the middle
of her head!

The farm five looked around and were confused.

Where could Unicorn have gone?

So they asked the little grey horse with a wavy tail like a lion of course and one big black top hat on her proud head. They asked in mime.

(Pointing to little grey horse) Have you…

(Pointing to eyes) seen…

(Miming a horn in the middle of the head) a unicorn?

And the little grey horse with a big black top hat on her proud head said:

"I have not seen any unicorn in the woods today."

Clyde was starting to smile because he had figured something out.

So he mimed a laugh and winked at the little grey horse that had…well you know.

"I must be off over Duck Mountain and on my way to Turtle Mountain and then on to Moose Mountain to see some friends," said the little grey one.

And off she went to the top of Duck Mountain. When she got there she turned to the farm five and said, "Goodbye for now."

It was right then that it happened.

A big gust of wind blued up.

Blued up?

I mean blew up.

And?

And knocked the hat right off the little grey horse.
What could you see where that hat used to be?

A horn!

One single sharp horn with a bright rainbow glow!

A horn right in the middle of her head! Oh you already
knew that.

What they all saw was a little grey horse,

> With a wavy tail like a lion of course.
> But what's most important for you to know?
> One diamond hard horn on her proud
>   head did grow,
> One single sharp horn with
>   a bright coloured glow!

IT'S THE UNICORN!

Faster than a gopher could dive into his hole, Unicorn turned and vanished over Duck Mountain.

The farm five just stared. They looked at where Unicorn had been, then they looked at each other, and as their eyes continued to look, they got madder and madder.

Since they didn't catch Unicorn, there would be no gold treasure for the farm.

Everyone, well, everyone but Clyde, blamed each other for the escape of Unicorn. They were so mad that everyone, well, everyone but Clyde…

Grabbed a voice out of the voice box…

Without even looking! Remember this part!

They were so mad that even with their voices back they would not say a single simple sound to each other. They slunk slowly and silently back to their farm.

It wasn't long after this; I heard it was this very morning, that the strangest, weirdest, silliest…well let me tell you.

It was just about time for the sun to peek up over the edge of the land. Red Rooster was flapping his wings and getting ready to sing his every morning song that we all know. You know the one I mean. You can do it yourself.

I call it the "er er er, er errrrrr" song. Or sometimes in other parts of the world where some roosters speak a different language it is called the "cock a doodle doodle song."

Red Rooster spoke "er" not "doodle". Just as the sun was bumping over the edge he flapped his wings one, two, three and said…

Moooooooo

Red Rooster said Moo?

When Susan and Darryl and Paul and David, the children on the farm, and their Dad were out doing their chores, Brown Cow turned and said…ER ER ER?

Spotted Dog chased Black Cat, round and round like any other morning and just as they faced each other in the corner of the barn, Spotted Dog said MEOW! MEOW?

Black Cat looked with a wrinkle in her nose and out of her mouth came…BOW! WOW?

And Clyde when he heard those words just laughed and laughed, the way any big horse would.

EEEEEEHEHEHEHE EEEEEHEHEHEHE EEHEEHE HE HE HA HA HA HA!

He laughed because he knew what happened and I think you do too. If you still wonder, go back five pages.

So if you are out driving some day on the prairies and you hear…

MOOOOOOOOOOOOO! Or even Moo.

Just smile, wink, and say to the people you are with:

"That rooster sure sings a good song."

The farm kept going even though the farmyard five did not catch Unicorn. It survived because everybody worked real hard or maybe Red Rooster scratched so deep he found a buried treasure. You decide what you think happened.

I can say for sure that The Last Unicorn on the Prairies is a true story, even if it isn't.

If you happen to be out on the prairie sometime let me know if you see a unicorn. She was last seen heading for Moose Mountain or was it Riding Mountain or maybe even the Cypress Hills.

Keep a look out. Maybe she wasn't the final last unicorn on the prairies.

You can't see if you don't look.

So if the sky doesn't fill up with polka dots. And…

The moon doesn't turn into an ice cream cone. And…

If your bed doesn't fly away with you. And…

If rabbits don't start playing hockey with coyotes…

Then I will tell you next time about all the ears and noses that fell off some kids and got stuck back on different kids and how mixed up their moms and dads and friends and uncles and aunts got. Until then, keep your nose and ears right where they are. If they get loose, hold them right where they are until I tell my next story to YOU.

THE END, for now